I0537852

That Kind of Love

Love

A Legacy Novella

J. Adams

J. Adams

Copyright © 2011 , 2015 J. Adams
Jewel of the West Publishing
All Rights Reserved
ISBN-13: 978-0615609690
ISBN-10: 0615609694

Library of Congress Control Number: 2012934239

To Loralee Evans,

Your day of grace is waiting in the wings.

Love you!

Though my world may be sightless,

my heart sees with absolute clarity.

Evangeline's Diary

Chapter 1

Salt Lake City, Utah

Andrew is dead.

And the sigh that escapes me is one of relief and gratitude. My blind eyes can make out the shadows of medical personnel moving around the hospital room, but I can't see Andrew's still features. I don't need to. There is a new silence in the room–the absence of irregular shallow breathing–for the next few moments. Then the soft sobs of his mother and mine dispel that silence.

With Andrew's death from undetected heart disease comes my freedom. The pressure of my parents to marry him has vanished and I feel as if a great weight has lifted, brightening my world like the sun coming out after a long, murky year of rain. I don't mean to be cold, but I've never loved Andrew. I've never even liked him. Nevertheless, my parents have been relentless in their desire to merge our family with Andrew Tanner's, to strategically combine two financial empires.

Andrew had been willing to put his own happiness aside, as well as mine, and go along for the ride. Had everything gone through, I would soon be trapped in a gilded prison I couldn't see, and would likely have died in. That death would have been a slow one, stealing my strength and my spirit a little each day until all of the things that have made me *me* disappeared, leaving an empty shell, my armor weakened, emotionally scarred and battered. Just like our parents, with Andrew, it had been all about the money. Love had nothing to do with it because, hey, let's face it. Who needs love?

"I do," I had told him. And he'd laughed. He actually laughed! It was never about our wants or desires. It was about our parents pimping us out to insure that the two companies went to bed together as

soon as possible. *"After all,"* Andrew had said, *"the end justifies the means. Blind, deaf or lame, it makes no difference to me."*

I offer my condolences to the Tanners, and then extend my cane and turn to leave. I imagine the mouths of the men silently opening and closing like fish lying on a shore in need of water, and the women shooting invisible fire darts with their eyes. Later on, I am sure my parents will dutifully harp about my cold and heartless exit, hoping to guilt me into showing the influential world the face of a grieving and heart-broken fiancée. But the days of me feeling guilty are long gone. If anything, I feel sympathy for the Tanner's loss. Andrew was their only son–their Golden Boy–the child they based their hopes and dreams on. His sisters are a different matter. Other than marrying rich men and breeding more sons to work in the family business, their two daughters are treated as if they are of no consequence. And since I'm an only child, my parents' dreams and ambitions for me are shot . . . unless a new financial opportunity emerges, an opportunity that will drive them to once again attempt to prostitute me for their gain. Of course, it figures since I'm not the daughter of their blood. I was adopted by them during one of their philanthropic trips down south. Boy, did they ever rack up brownie points for adopting a token black baby, and a blind one at that!

Will I always be worth so little to them?

However, I have been given a healthy dose of strength, and I will no longer let my parents–Mr. and Mrs. What Can You Do For Me Patton–run my life. Thanks to the good Lord, I am in charge now, and I am open and ready to receive the kind of love, and the kind of life, He has in store for me. In God's eyes I am worth more. I don't know how much more, but definitely more than the value my parents place on my existence.

The trust fund I inherited four years ago on my twenty-first birthday has given me the financial freedom to live on my own in a downtown high rise condominium that I own outright. And the money I earn giving violin and cello lessons takes care of my needs. I guess you could say I have it all.

Yes, you could say that . . . but you would be wrong. Until now, the thing I have desired most–what I have *needed* most–has eluded me.

I smile, sensing a coming change. A change bringing a life that has always been mine. A change I have been prepared for, and one I am now ready to receive.

* * *

Treviso, Italy

Fixing his teary, emerald gaze on the large granite headstone bearing his grandparents' names, Adagio Phillip St. John the third removes his sunglasses and heaves a deep sigh. It seems sunglasses have become a part of him, a shield and a mask.

It has been a month since he lost the two dearest people in the world to him, and his heart still carries a fierce ache. How he misses them! They had always been an example to him of how he wants to live his life, and the love they shared was truly a thing to behold. His mother and father share a deep love as well, but what his grandmother and grandfather had between them was indescribable.

Adagio is in his early thirties and has yet to marry. And he will never marry until he finds someone he can share that kind of love with–the kind his grandparents shared. He refuses to settle. His sisters constantly tell him he is too picky, but his grandparents knew different. They truly understood him.

While he has always been called Dagio by the family to avoid confusion, his grandmother always called him Young Adagio because he was a mirror image of her husband in his thirties. Frequently Adagio sat with his grandmother looking through photo albums, and each time they came to a picture of his grandfather, Adagio was amazed at how much he looked like him, even more so than his father, Phillip. It was uncanny.

Blinking tears onto his face, Adagio pulls a folded piece of paper from his back pocket. It is a letter he found inside his grandmother's journal along with two keys. She had given the book to him the day before she passed away. Tearfully opening the journal on the day of her funeral, Adagio had been surprised when the envelope fell from between the pages. It was addressed to him. A fresh tear stain appears on the paper as he unfolds it and again reads his dear *nonna's* final words to him.

My, Dearest Young Adagio,

By now I am most likely gone from this earth, but I'm never far away from you. I know you are hurting just as your grandfather is. I'm so sorry to cause you pain and would have spared you from it if I could. But the pain will one day fade and healing will come.

Since the day you were born, you have always been my light and my joy, and your grandfather's as well. And even though I will not be there to watch you find love and raise your own children, I will be watching from afar. You are probably thinking, "Yeah, right, Nonna, I'll never find anyone like you and will probably die a lonely old man." And don't try to deny it because I know you.

This part again draws a wide smile from him. She really did know him well.

Now, I know you recognize the keys and there is no need to tell you what they are for. When your grandfather and I pondered what to do with the old house in the states, the answer quickly came to us. No one understands the importance of the house and how much it means to us more than you. You and your grandfather share the same heart, which is why you could always read me so well.

So this is what I would like you to do. Pack your things and move to Salt Lake. The move will be painful for your parents and they will miss you greatly, but you won't be gone long. This is a necessary step because your life won't truly start until you are where you belong. Remember what your grandfather told you about looking for love and finding it in God's time? Well, my dear boy, it looks like your life up to this point has mirrored his. And as surely as he found the love of his life, you will, too. I have a good feeling about this, and you know your nonna is never wrong, right? Shake your head.

Chuckling, Adagio shakes his head no.

Adagio, I love you more than I can say and I always will. I am proud of the man you have become. Now go live your life, and be happy. Remember, I will never be far away.

Love,

Nonna

P.S. Remember to take the ring. You remember where it is, right?

Yes, Nonna, I remember. He pulls her emerald engagement ring from his pocket, pondering the story behind it. It was given to his grandfather by his own mother to give to his future wife. His grandfather had taken it everywhere he went, never guessing he would eventually be placing it on the finger of the woman who had become his best friend.

And now it is my turn.

Folding the letter, Adagio puts it back in his pocket and wipes his eyes. He looks at the headstone one last time. "I love you, *Nonna,* and you, *Nonno,*" he whispers. "And I will try to make you both proud." He smiles, then puts his sunglasses back on and walks away, charting a course toward his new life.

Chapter 2

Be reasonable, Evangeline! You are expected to be there!"

Mother and Father have been harping all morning on my decision not to attend Andrew's funeral this afternoon. I am annoyed and angry, but most of all, hurt. "You haven't heard a thing I've said, have you?"

"You must come!" Mother repeats. "There is still a chance to close the merger. We must show a united front. The Tanners, as well as the others attending must see your sorrow. It can only help."

Tears sting my eyes, but I refuse to let them come.

Each word that spills from their lips only increases the pain I've carried inside for most of my adult life. "You still don't get it. It no longer matters to me what people expect. I did not love Andrew and I won't go and falsely portray a grieving almost-widow. I'm done pretending."

"Now listen . . ."

"No, you listen!" I interrupt my father. I'm finished listening to their careless and unfeeling rants. "You have made my life a living hell and I am done letting you bully and walk all over me. Yes, I am blind, but I am not stupid. I am twenty-five years old and I have my own life. It's *my* life, not yours. I have always given you power over me, but no more. It stops here and now." I close my eyes and rub my temples, trying to relieve the ache in my head. "You know, I can't remember a time either of you were ever there for me, other than when you were coaxing me to do your bidding. All you do is use, use, use. When you look at me, you don't even see me, you see something to be used for your gain. I'm blind, yet I see clearer than you do. You don't love me and I doubt you ever have. In fact, why did you bother to adopt me in the first place?"

Father sputters, "How dare you speak to us this way! We have given you everything! You have lived a life most people can only dream of living."

"How can you be so ungrateful?" Mother cries.

"Oh, I'm grateful for the comfortable life I've had. But you see, that's just it. You gave me everything except what I have needed most: the simple love of a parent. That would have been worth more than all the money filling your bank accounts."

Father's face is an angry crimson. "If it hadn't been for us adopting you, you would probably be living out on the streets somewhere, following in the footsteps of your drug addict mother. After all, that's why you were born blind."

Wow! "And I thought you couldn't sink any lower, Father. I was mistaken." I shake my head sadly. "I will always love you both and be grateful for the life I've been given, but from now on I will be living my life for me and God, and no one else."

In self-preservation, I harden my heart against Mother's dramatic whimpers. She knows how to use that tactic well and I cannot allow it to affect me the way it used to. Closing my eyes, I inhale the expensive smell of my childhood home. This will most likely be the last time I stand inside it for a long while. Saying nothing more, I swallow my emotions, unfold my cane, and make my way through the entryway and out to my waiting taxi.

* * *

Standing in the doorway of the living room, Adagio visualizes the memories his grandparents shared in the old house. From the moment he arrived yesterday, he has felt the essence of their love for one another in every corner of the place.

He walks over to the baby grand piano and lightly runs fingers over the smooth surface, remembering the times he sat on the bench next to his grandmother and played duets. He had been a fast learner and she was always generous in her praise. This room had been her favorite place in the house. It was also in this room that his grandfather realized he was in love with her.

Sitting on the bench, he revisits the conversation he had with his grandfather in this room as he shared those memories.

"We were just friends, but I started spending more and more time with Nonna. I hated being away from her. I thought about her constantly, and I tried staying away a couple of times, just to see if the feelings would leave me if he didn't spend so much time around her. But guess what? I couldn't go a whole day without seeing her because I needed to be near her.

"Every moment we were together, I watched her every move. I would look at her face and wonder what she was thinking. Whenever she left the room, I counted the minutes until she came back, and when she did, my heart always skipped a beat. Every time she looked at me or touch my hand, I melted.

"Her grief over losing her first husband wasn't as painful anymore, but I started missing the opportunities I had to hold her when she needed comforting. I missed her softness against me and, the fragrance of her hair. I loved breathing it in because it was so her. I had grown used to the way her body fit against me, and my arms felt so empty. I loved the way her eyes sparkled whenever I came over, and the way her silky voice sounded when she said my name. Being with her was like coming home. It was the first time I had ever felt that way about someone. My need for her was exciting and frightening at the same time.

"But this is the moment I knew I was in love with her. The week before, I went to find Nonna to tell her lunch was ready. I was standing right in that doorway when I found her standing in front of the window staring out at the city. She was very pregnant, but she was still the most beautiful thing I had ever seen. I just stood there staring at her, unable to pull my eyes away. I couldn't even move. It was like something was keeping *me in that spot. I just kept thinking, "She's so beautiful! She is just so beautiful!*

"And at that moment, I wanted to walk over to her, take her in my arms and kiss her passionately, and never let her go. My feelings were intense and the lyrics to the music softly playing on the stereo suddenly hit me hard. It was one of my favorite songs because it was about finding home in the one you love, and it stirred my emotions so much, I could hardly breathe. Longing filled me and all I could think about was how much I wanted her to be mine. I had never needed someone so much.

"I lost track of time just watching her. Then she turned and smiled at me and my heart was completely hers. Because I wasn't sure of her feelings, I was afraid to act on mine. So I decided to wait, and as you can see, I didn't wait long. We soon came to know we were meant to be together. She was my whole life. And she still is."

"And I'm sure she is even now, *Nonno*," Adagio whispers, feelings his grandparents close by. A sudden urge to view the spot where his grandparents were married draws him through the kitchen and out to the back yard. Taking in the view, he pictures their wedding just as his grandmother described it.

"We were married in the backyard beneath an arched, rose-covered trellis. I wore a slim-fitting, ivory-colored, silk and lace dress, and a friend had styled my hair in an intricate up-do that was a work of art. As soon as your grandfather saw me, he told me over and over I was beautiful. He

never took his eyes off me. And he was so handsome in his dark blue Armani suit. To me there wasn't a more perfect looking man in the world. He was a heart breaker and he was all mine.

"It was a small wedding with only a few guests. That's the way we wanted it, and it was perfect.

"When we exchanged vows and were pronounced husband and wife, everything changed for me. He was everything I could ever want."

Adagio laughs. "And I'm sure he still is, *Nonna.* I can see you nodding your head now." Heaving a deep sigh, he wipes the moisture from his eyes and heads back into the house to make a grocery list. He had eaten out yesterday, but now that he is unpacked and settled, he is ready to do some cooking and add the familiar scent of home to the place.

Chapter 3

Two weeks later

Carrying a shopping bag in one hand and my cane in the other, I relish the warm breeze against my face as I cut through the Main Street plaza and head home. The area is usually busy on Saturday afternoons and today is no exception. My ears pick up several different languages as tourists walk the plaza and the grounds of the Salt Lake Temple, snapping pictures and talking with young women serving as their guides. I've always loved this area of downtown.

Just as I'm exiting the plaza, someone rushes by

me, knocking me down. As my knees hit the pavement, my cane goes one way and my bag the other.

"Sorry!" a teenage voice calls from a distance, which tells me he was either on skates or a skateboard. Both are against the rules and not allowed on the plaza grounds. Ignoring the pain of my scraped knees on the pavement, I send up a silent prayer for help and begin to feel around for my cane. A second later, a gentle hand touches mine.

"Let me help you." Giving the owner of the heavily-accented voice my hand, he helps me to my feet. "I'll get your things." He starts to pull his hand from mine and my grip tightens. My pacing and sense of direction are off, leaving me totally disoriented. "It's all right," the deep voice says kindly. "Just stay still. I'm right here, okay?"

"Okay," I manage to answer, slightly upset by the whole ordeal. I've never had to depend on anyone for anything, and here I am, unable to shift back into comfort mode.

"Here is your cane," he says. "Now just tell me where you need to go and I'll carry your bag and walk with you."

"You don't need to do that." The protest comes out stronger than I intended. "I mean, thank you for your help, but if you can just point me in the right direction, I will be fine. You don't need to help me further."

"I know, but I want to. All right?" When I say nothing, he adds, "And since you were most likely raised to never talk to strangers, especially some scruffy Italian guy who has only been in the country for a couple of weeks and wants to walk a beautiful woman home, just so he can spend a few more minutes with her and maybe learn her name, you are probably cautious. But then again, if she asks him his name and gives him hers, they won't be total strangers any longer."

I try to hold it back, but a wide smile quickly breaks across my face. "I think that is about the smoothest line I have ever heard."

"Really? Oh, good. I practiced it for all of five seconds and I hoped it would go over well."

"Wow, only five seconds, huh? I would never have guessed," I tease, the warmth in his voice putting me even more at ease.

"Thank you for the compliment. But the question

is, *did* it go over well?"

"It did," I answer with a laugh.

"Oh, wonderful!" he says and I laugh at his exaggerated sigh of relief. "Now, if you will give me your hand and navigate, I will get you where you need to go. But first I must introduce myself. My name is Adagio St. John."

"Please to meet you, Mr. St. John."

"And?"

"And what?" I tease.

"You are . . .?"

"Oh, Evangeline."

"I am pleased to meet you, Evangeline." The way he says my name . . . I've never heard it like that. His voice is like a caress. "Are you ready?"

I can't believe I'm about to do this! Lifting my face to him, I put out my hand. As he weaves his long fingers through mine, I marvel that it should feel so right. "I've never done anything like this in my life. I mean, you are a complete stranger."

"Not anymore," he says warmly.

"Thanks for reminding me."

"My pleasure."

Chapter 4

When they reach Evangeline's apartment building, Adagio is reluctant to release her hand, and judging by the warmth he senses from her, her feelings are the same.

"Thanks for your help," she tells him. "I couldn't have made it without you."

Adagio grins. "Oh, I think you would have eventually been just fine. That independent streak of yours would not have allowed you to give up."

She smiles. "You know me well. I guess we really aren't strangers, are we?"

No, I think I've known you my whole life. "Indeed we are not. Which means I am welcome to come and see you again, right?"

When her smile widens, he officially admits it to himself; he's a goner. Those beautiful, laughing brown eyes and that irresistibly-full smiling mouth could melt the coldest of hearts. During their walk to her place, he'd stolen countless glances at her, and her every feature is burned in his memory, never to be erased–her smooth caramel skin, her shoulder-length, auburn tightly-curled hair, and that amazing spirit. She radiates warmth that he would love to curl up into forever.

"Since we are such great friends now, I guess so," she answers. "But . . . you have to agree to indulge in one of my favorite card games."

"Cards, huh? I think I can do that. I'll even bring a six pack of root-beer. How's that?"

"That sounds great. And I'll provide hot wings and potato skins. I mean, what's a card game without game food?"

"Not much of a card game," he answers, grinning. "So, how is tomorrow?"

"I teach music until four. We can do it then."

"What do you teach?"

"Violin, cello and percussion. The last is always done at the student's home. Wouldn't want the neighbors to run me out of the place."

Adagio laughs. "I can understand that." He smiles, thinking of *Nonna*. "My grandmother was gifted in music as well. She taught me to play the piano."

"Really?" Evangeline says, a grin splitting her adorable face. "I have a Clavinova. We will have to collaborate a little while you're here."

"I look forward to making music with you," he says in a simpering tone, drawing a snort from her, and a fit of laughter erupts between them. "I'll see you tomorrow then."

"See you tomorrow." He gives her hand another squeeze and she returns the gesture. He releases it again and opens the door for her.

"Thank you again," she says softly.

"You're welcome." He stands outside the door and doesn't move until she is on the elevator and the doors close. *And there goes my heart,* he muses. *Take care of it, angel.*

Heading back the way he came, Adagio can't stop grinning. *Was I even alive before today?* He imagines hearing *Nonna's* voice saying, *"Of course not!"* Chuckling inwardly, he removes his sunglasses, tossing them in a nearby garbage can. He no longer needs them.

He whistles as he heads home.

* * *

Closing my apartment door, I lean back against it and sigh, unable to believe today's experience. What I've done today would likely appall some people. My parents would definitely think I've gone over the edge. But that's the beauty of no longer allowing what they think to control me.

What started out as a terrible experience turned into one of the most amazing things that has ever happened to me. Crawling around on my hands and knees in public, trying to locate my cane and bag, could have been totally embarrassing, but the moment I felt the touch of Adagio's gentle hand on mine and heard his accented voice softly say, "Let me help you," I felt a warmth unlike anything I've ever experienced. I tell myself it had only been because he was so kind to me, but I know it is more than that.

He's a stranger to me, I continue to argue. But he isn't. It is like I've rediscovered an old friend I haven't seen in a long time. I flex the fingers of the hand he held as we walked, pondering how empty that hand feels now.

Get a grip, girl! I heave a deep sigh and put my purchases away, putting Adagio out of my mind for now. At least, I try to.

Chapter 5

"Uno!" I call, putting down a Braille-marked draw two card. Adagio puts down a red card, which is what I need. I place my final card on his, chuckling at his cry of disbelief.

"I give up! How many hands is that?"

"Five to your one."

"And it was by sheer luck I won that one. Good thing I've been dealing every hand. With these cleverly-marked cards, I wouldn't have stood a chance."

"Yes, you would have. I would've given you a handicap and let you win one or two. Maybe."

"Well, I appreciate the thought."

"No problem," I say, enjoying our playful bantering. "Now I think I'm brave enough to try the Tiramisu you brought."

"I promise you will love it," Adagio assures me, helping to put the leftover hot wings and potato skins away. "It was my grandfather's recipe. My father taught me to make it when I was ten."

"Ten? Seriously?"

"Completely. When I turned eighteen I started working in the family restaurant as a chef. I learned much from my father and grandfather."

"That must have been a great experience for you." I try to keep envy from creeping into my voice, but it is hard. Everything I know about cooking, and tending a home period, I learned from Ruth and her daughter, Kathryn. They have been the cook and housekeeper of Mother and Father's home since I was a toddler. And since my mother spared very little attention for me, the two kind women took me under their wings and I grew to love them like family.

"It was," Adagio answers. I can tell by the tone of his voice he is trying to be sensitive to my feelings, and

I appreciate it more than he knows. As I shared bits of my life with him earlier, including my parents using me for their gain, I could feel his compassion for me. It had been a relief having him here to talk to, and to actually have a friend who cares means the world.

"Do you plan to resume your chef position one day?"

"Maybe one day, but not now. As much as I love cooking, it isn't a career choice at the moment, just a relaxing hobby. Music is my career."

"Singer or songwriter?"

He snorts. "Neither. I'm a composer."

"Cool!" I say, impressed. "Have you composed many works?"

"I've done a few." The modesty ringing in his voice tells me he has done more than a few, and has probably done well in his career. "Okay, when we finish eating dessert, the Clavinova is yours."

"If you insist," he whines playfully.

* * *

As we come to the end of an amazing evening, I'm a little saddened that he has to go. I've never had so much fun with someone. This is the first time in years that I have not felt alone. Even though we have only known each other for a couple of days, I can honestly say he has become a dear friend to me, and for the first time ever, I mourn the absence of my sight. My expression must betray my thoughts because he notices my distress immediately.

"What is it?" Adagio asks as I walk him to the door.

"Nothing," I say, trying to smile without much success.

"Hey," he says, taking my hands in his. "What is it?"

Feeling the threatening sting of tears, I furiously blink them back. "I just wish I could see you."

"You can." There is a slight crack in his voice.

I allow him to guide my hands to his face. As soon as they make contact with his skin, I smile, warmth spreading through me as my fingers move from his whiskered cheeks, lightly tracing his closed eyes, his brows. His lashes are enviably long. I allow my hands to get lost in his hair, hearing him draw in a breath in response. My fingers slowly travel down the masculine bridge of his nose, then to his broad, muscular shoulders, and finally back up to his full lips, saving the best for last. I slowly drop my hands and smile. "How tall are you?"

"Six-foot-two," he breathes.

"What color are your eyes?"

"Green."

"And your hair?"

"Black."

"You aren't just handsome . . . you're beautiful."

He takes my hands again, drawing me close. "You are beautiful." His voice is a whisper. "The most beautiful thing I have ever seen."

I swallow hard against the lump in my throat. "No one has ever told me that before," I say, finding it hard to believe his words. Even when Andrew was alive, he never told me I was beautiful. I feel the warmth of Adagio's hands as he takes my face in them and tears spill unchecked down my cheeks. My heart pounds as his shadow draws closer. When his face is close enough for me to feel his breath fanning my lips, there is a knock at the door. He softly presses a kiss to my forehead and moves away. I take a moment to compose myself.

The voice that greets me when I finally open the door is the last one I expected to hear.

"I need to talk to you," Father says, abruptly pushing past me. The over-powering smell of alcohol follows him.

"Father, this isn't a good time for me right now."

"Well, it's the perfect time for *me*." There is no kindness in his voice, but then again, there never has been. "Thanks to your coldness, the Tanners are pulling out of the deal."

Evidently, Adagio is out of sight. That he is still here is comforting to me. "I'm sorry the merger fell through, but I am not to blame."

"Oh, you better believe you are. But I'm about to tell you how you will make it up to me."

Chapter 6

Standing in Evangeline's bedroom looking through the cracked doorway, Adagio's heart goes out to her. In the ten seconds her father has been here, every single thing she'd told Adagio about the cold-hearted man is confirmed. He has never witnessed anything so sad or seen someone so cruel. Taking in her father's disheveled appearance and the unsteadiness of his movements, Adagio is sure the man has been drinking. He continues to silently listen, watching in complete incredulity, unable to believe what he is hearing.

The man is a demon! He has no soul. He's not even human!

* * *

"You are kidding me! You want me to what?"

"You heard me, girl. My new perspective partner has a penchant for you so-called women of color. It's about time you earned the good life I've provided for you. Just keep him happy until we seal the deal. Who knows, you might grow to like it and want to make it permanent. This is what I have been grooming you for, Evangeline. And since you can't see the man, it shouldn't make a difference what he looks like."

By now I am shaking so badly with hurt and anger, I can hardly think. I have been right all along. This is the value my father places on me. Other than being the Mercury Technologies company whore, I'm not worth much else.

"Does Mother know about this?"

"I don't answer to your mother. I am the head of my house. My word is law, so she has no choice but to support me. Besides, I take care of her well enough."

"Adopted or not, I am still your daughter. How can you treat me this way?"

"Because I *own* you, that's how. And a good daughter would be obedient and not give me any lip."

I slip my shaking hands into the pockets of my jeans, having no luck in steadying them. "Father, I would like you to leave now." I try to keep my voice calm. "And please don't come back." When I hear his angry heaves, I move away from him, a cold fear entering me.

"I will leave when I am good and ready! Who do you think you are, the African Queen or something? It is because of me you even have all of this." He swings his arms around the living room. "Do you really think you can order me around like some whipping boy? If you do, then think again. I guess I'm going to have to show you who is in charge."

* * *

Before the drunk man's hand can make contact with Evangeline's face, Adagio catches his arm, spinning him around. "I wouldn't do that if I were you." There is ice in his voice. He watches her father's eyes widen.

"Who in the hell are you and what are you doing in my daughter's apartment?"

"I am Evangeline's friend, and why I am here is none of your business." He glances at Evangeline. "Are you all right?" When she tearfully nods, his piercing eyes move back to her father. "I suggest you leave now. Or do you need a little help?"

Her father slowly smiles. "Oh, I see how it is. Sleeping with her, are you? You're not the first, you know?"

An emotional gasp escapes Evangeline. "How can you say something like that?"

"Well, it's true, isn't it? And I'm sure your foreign playboy here can teach you something new. Your experience will come in handy for Mercury. I can put you both on the payroll."

"Get out!" she yells. "Just get out!"

He moves toward her. "Why you little tramp! I'll . . ."

In two swift moves, Adagio has the man's arms twisted behind his back. "You are seriously delusional. Not just delusional, you are sick."

"Get your hands off me!"

"I will," Adagio says, yanking him toward the door. "Evangeline, would you mind?" He watches her nervously move to the door and quickly open it. Releasing her father's arms, Adagio pitches him against the hallway wall and slams the door shut.

* * *

I am shaking badly, and I can't seem to stop. Only when Adagio's warm, muscular arms come around me do I begin to calm. Listening to Father ranting outside the door, I am stung by each obscenity he yells at me. "I'm sorry," I whisper against his chest.

"Hey, you have nothing to apologize for. *I'm* sorry for all he has put you through."

Adagio's embrace steals away the pain, and his gentle spirit warms me to the core. "Thank you for being here. I don't want to think about what might have happened had I been alone."

"You will never have to worry about that. I will always be here for you." He draws back a little and I feel the warmth of his gaze on my face. "I don't trust your father. We need to get you out of here for a few days."

"But where would I go?"

"To my place. You can have your choice of the eight empty bedrooms. And don't say no, just leave your independent streak here and let someone take care of you for a while."

Swallowing against the rising emotion, I nod. "I can't believe I'm not even safe in my own home anymore, and that the danger is my father is just unreal."

He says nothing else, but pulls me further into himself. Tightening my arms around his waist, I silently soak in the safety of his protective embrace.

* * *

Kathryn Patton is reading in bed when her husband staggers into the room. He wreaks of alcohol. Again.

"Where have you been?"

"Where do you think? I went to try and talk some sense into the tramp that is your daughter."

"I thought we agreed it was pointless to try anymore."

"I didn't agree to anything. You might be ready to give up what we've worked so hard for, but I am not."

"Of course I'm not giving up, George. But merging with another company is not a matter of life and death. Let's just cut our losses and continue to go it alone.

Mercury is doing well enough."

He turns a wild-eyed stare to her and her heart jumps. She has never seen him like this. "You have no idea what you're talking about, so just shut up and leave the thinking to me!" He staggers back to the door. "I'll sleep in the den."

As her husband leaves the room, Kathryn presses a shaky hand to her mouth, contemplating how things between them have gone from bad to worse. Something is definitely wrong. George is keeping something from her. Not that he hasn't kept secrets in the past, only they really were not secrets because she knows them all. She is very much aware of his late night trips to Wendover, and she knows he usually isn't alone on those jaunts. She feels the subtle glances of female employees whenever she goes into the office. She has also watched those same employees exit her husband's office, disheveled, avoiding eye contact. Yes, these are things she has always turned a blind eye to and willingly ignored.

No, there is something else going on, and Kathryn has a feeling that when she discovers the truth, things are only going to get worse.

Chapter 7

I'm trying to think of a time when my father showed me any affection. Sadly, I can't. Not even one." I sigh, snuggling deeper in Adagio's embrace. Our words are spoken softly and I feel safe and at home in his cozy living room.

"I'm sorry your father deprived you of basic human affection, something that should automatically come with being a parent. What about your mother?"

I think a moment. "There were maybe a few times when I was younger, but not much more. She kind of went along with my father when it came to showing love. I don't think she meant to, but . . ." I mentally search for an excuse but can't find one.

"Your trials have made you stronger."

"I don't feel strong. Sometimes I feel far from it."

"You are stronger than you think, angel. And I promise you will get through this."

Raising my eyes, I try to study his blurred outline, wishing so badly that I could see him, if only for a moment. But then again, a moment would not be enough, and I would most likely be worse off, having been gifted that ability only to have the picture of him taken away. "How do you know I'm strong?" The sensation of his lips pressing against my forehead sends warmth through my whole body.

Instead of answering, he says, "I need to get something. I'll be right back, all right?"

"Okay."

He returns a moment later. "I would like to read something to you from my grandmother's journal. She had some major trials with her family. She was raised by an alcoholic mother and a father who molested her for years. Her self-medicating turned into a drug and alcohol problem, but she was finally able to change her life. The rest of her family would have nothing to do with her for a long time."

"Wow! What a painful life. I can't imagine what she went through."

"My grandmother was a strong woman, which is why I wanted to read this to you."

"All right." I turned to him, anxious to know about the woman Adagio was so close to.

In my twenty-two years of life, I have dealt with things no one should have to. Having been raised by an alcoholic mother and an abusive father, my childhood was miserable. From the age of six to twelve years old, when other children were laughing and playing and sharing secrets with their friends, I was a woman-child, barely surviving and telling my secrets to no one. In the afternoons after school when I should have been out playing, I sat in my bedroom, listening to the screams of my mother as my father beat her. And at night while other children were sleeping, I was forced to endure the sickening presence of my father in my room as he defiled me.

One day my mother finally packed our things while my father was at work and we moved from Charlotte back to her hometown of Asheville. Unfortunately, it was too little, too late, because I was permanently scarred. And it didn't help that every man who entered into our home and lived with my mother thought I was part of the deal.

Throughout my life I felt dirty, cheap, and alone. I had no one to share my painful burdens. Later in life, I made decisions that only added to my misery, bringing even more shame upon me.

There were days and nights of endless partying, each one filled with drugs, alcohol, and sometimes immorality. When I was younger, my father told me repeatedly that I was worthless and only good for one thing in life. It seemed his comments found a permanent place in both my mind and my heart. My father foresaw my future and had helped as much as he could to make that future happen. But I know the choices had been my own, just as the choice to finally change my life had been.

I remember the day I made the decision to abandon the self-destructive lifestyle. I had just gotten home from work, I was tired from waiting on table *after table, and I was looking forward to a tall can of beer and some rest. I had*

just sat down when there was a knock at the door.

When I opened the door, there was a braid-wearing teenage girl donning

heavy makeup, a dirty mini skirt, and scuffed up high heels—one of them

broken. My first words were, "Sorry, no customers at this house."

She gave me a teary smile and replied, "I'm not looking for a customer . . .

I'm looking for a way out."

My heart had instantly gone out to her. I knew the life she'd lived and

what she'd suffered before reaching this point in her life. I knew, because I had

been there, myself. I invited her in and listened as she talked. My suspicions

about her abusive childhood were confirmed. I fed her and gave her some clothes

to change into. Then I took the tips I'd made that day from my purse, called a

cab, took her to the bus station, and put her on a bus to Raleigh to go and live

with her aunt. When I finally arrived back home, I sat on the sofa, closed my eyes

and cried. Nothing I'd ever done in my life left me feeling as much peace as that

one act had.

I immediately threw away all of the alcohol in the apartment and vowed to never take another drink, pop another pill, or smoke another joint for the rest of my life. I stopped partying and made a commitment to change my life. I was determined to do this, despite family members and friends telling me I would never change. I really had no support from anyone except the counselor assigned to me when I enrolled in a free substance abuse program. No one I knew would let go of the past. I couldn't either. I couldn't escape it because it was constantly being thrown back in my face.

Moving to Utah to stay with Jessica was the best decision I ever made. It wasn't until then that my life truly started.

"Wow!" I whisper again, a tear slipping down my cheek. "I just can't imagine going through something so painful."

"But you are," Adagio says, caressing my cheek. "The trial is different, but I would guess the pain is about the same." I hear him turning the pages. "Now I would like to read another entry she wrote years later.

This afternoon I took a moment and again pondered my life and how far

I have come. If someone had told me ten years ago that I would one day be living in Italy and married to a painfully handsome Italian man, I would have considered that person out of his or her mind. Then I probably would have offered the person a drink to help them regain their sanity, because that was how I always handled things back then. A drink and an occasional drug to go with it could cure anything. Thinking about that part of my life always makes me shudder. Back then, I could never have fathomed living such a life now. I did not know my worth then, but I do now. And I know my worth to God.

I'm so grateful for these times of reflection because I need to remember where I've been and how far I have come. And though the past is full of painful memories, I will never let myself forget. I can't, because every trial I overcame served to bring me here, sharing my life with a man I love more than life—a man I can't imagine not being with, and one that I could never be without.

"I wish I could have known her," I say, wiping my tears. "I wish I could have known both of your grandparents."

"So do I," he says, pressing a hand to my cheek once more.

Needing the comfort of his arms, I rest my weary head

against his shoulder and he pulls me snugly against him. Closing my eyes, I think of Adagio's grandmother, wishing with all my heart I had her strength. I tell myself that one day I will.

Chapter 8

I have been staying at Adagio's home for the past few days and I've enjoyed every minute I have been able to spend with him. To make things easier, he'd chosen the guest room on the main floor for me. After walking me around the entire floor a few times, I finally know the layout enough that I'm able to move around freely without bumping into things.

I brought my violin and cello with me, and we spend an hour or so each day immersed in music, playing duets on Adagio's baby grand, or accompanying each other, him on the piano and me on strings. The result is both stirring and beautiful. I don't think my playing will ever be the same, not without his beautiful notes present, the combination of the two swelling in the silence.

My cell phone has been ringing on and off throughout each day. I cringe every time I see my parents' number on the caller ID, and by the end of the day I usually wind up deleting at least fifty messages from my father. Some are civil while others are vulgar and hateful. I wasn't aware my father knew such a disgusting vocabulary, and his liberal use of it takes a toll on my spirit. Each night Adagio holds me and I cry myself to sleep, only to awaken the next morning tucked safely in bed. His tender care makes me love him more each day. And that is truly what I feel. I have yet to speak the words. Part of me is afraid to. For now, I will keep them to myself.

* * *

Two days later when I check my voice mail, there is an emotional message from Mother.

"Evangeline, it's me. Your father is in the hospital. He was driving drunk and hit someone head on. He is on life support and isn't expected to make it. Oh,

Evangeline, please come. I can't do this alone. Please come."

* * *

Adagio's hand is clasped tightly in mine as I enter the hospital room, and I am grateful. There is no way I would have agreed to come without him here for moral support. His strength buoys me up and gives me courage. It is startling how much I have grown to depend on him during this past week.

Pressing his lips to my ear, he whispers, "Your mother is sitting by the bed."

The room is silent except for the ventilator breathing for Father. I can feel Mother's gaze on me and it's a little unnerving. For a change, I guess I will need to speak first.

"When did it happen?"

"Last night," comes Mother's soft answer. I hear the strain in her voice. "He had gone back to your place several times, determined to see you. He finally decided to call the police and report your 'abduction.'" When my eyes widen in incredulous surprise, she goes on. "I managed to talk him out of it, convincing him that making a false report like that is a serious thing and he would be putting himself in a bad situation, which would not look good for the company."

I know she senses my relief. I don't know what I would have done if Adagio had been picked up and thrown in jail for abducting me, when nothing was further from the truth. "Thank you for stopping him." Though she is silent, I sense her acknowledgment.

"Last night I received a call from someone in accounting. I was told the truth about your father and why he has become so obsessed with gaining a partnership with almost anyone he can." She hesitates a moment. "It seems he has been embezzling money from Mercury with the help of an accounting employee who is no longer there. He has been using the money to pay off gambling debts I had no idea he acquired."

That explains a lot. He had been willing to sacrifice me, his own daughter, to pay off his gambling debts. Only someone with no love in their heart could do something that low and degrading. Everything inside me wants to burrow myself in a corner somewhere and cry my eyes out. The gentle squeeze of Adagio's hand comforts me and assures me of his unwavering support.

"What happened?" I ask, prompting her to continue.

"When I confronted him about practically ruining the company, he became even angrier and said he was going out again to find you. I told him to just leave you alone, that we had hurt you enough, but . . ."

"The bruise on your cheek is the result," Adagio finishes for her, surprising me. I wait for Mother to speak again. Her silence touches a small part of my heart. I swore I would never let that happen again.

"How are you?" I finally ask.

"Oh, I'm . . . well, I . . ."

Her voice breaks, and so does my heart in her behalf. Moving in the direction of her voice, I put out my hand. The room isn't light enough for me to make out her shadow. A few seconds later she timidly takes it and I feel her shaking.

"I'm sorry," she whispers. Oh, Evangeline, I'm so sorry for everything. I will regret how we've treated you–how *I've* treated you–every day for the rest of my life. I held back so much from you. I have a lot to answer to, and make up for." Her gentle hand on my cheek surprises me and fills me with a longed-for sense of joy. "I promise I will do everything I can to try to earn your trust, your respect, and your love. I know it won't be easy, but . . ." Her voice cracks and she says nothing more.

I don't need to hear anything more. And I don't try to stop the tears this time. I allow them to run unchecked down my face. My step forward meets hers and we embrace. In the cradle of my mother's arms, I release years of hurt, anger and neglect, my heart opening to her after a long season of keeping it under lock and key.

Drawing back, I again feel the touch of Mother's hand gently pressing against my cheek. "I promise to never abandon you again."

I smile. "I promise you the same."

* * *

A warm tear trails down Adagio's face as he witnesses the sweet and tender, long-awaited reunion of the woman his heart and soul cries out for, and the mother she thought she'd lost forever. Watching them share smiles and maternal embraces, healing each other after so much hurt, fills a part of him that has been empty since losing his grandparents. And when

Evangeline's mother moves to Adagio, takes his hand and says, "My name is Kathryn and I'm pleased to meet you," he truly feels blessed.

Chapter 9

One week later.

Rocking the porch swing gently, Adagio holds Evangeline close and offers what comfort he can. Her father's graveside service was yesterday and most of the people in attendance were Mercury employees. It seems her father burned a lot of bridges over the past year, and the words spoken over his grave had been few.

Evangeline had spent most of today with her mother, going through her father's things, packing up and storing what they would keep, and loading the rest into her mother's car to take to the homeless shelter. Kathryn will be tied up the rest of the week, trying to repair the damage at Mercury, so now it is just Adagio and Evangeline.

As the skies darken, a street light comes on at the end of the block, but he and Evangeline are shadowed from the rest of the world. Caressing her face while holding her snugly in his arms, emotion wells up inside him. Unable to resist, he presses his lips against her ear and whispers, "I love you, Evangeline. You don't have to love me back right now, or say the words if you don't feel the same, but I just needed you to know."

* * *

Drawing back a little, I smile, touching his face, his lips. The words come easy. "I do love you, Adagio. More than I ever dreamed I could love someone." My skin tingles at the touch of his fingers slowly caressing every part of my face, ending with the feather-light tracing of my lips. He draws me closer, holding me so closely, I can feel the beat of his heart, its rhythm matching my own.

"I believe you. Would you like to know why?"

"Yes."

"I believe you because your eyes have never allowed you to look upon me, yet you see me better than anyone. You love exclusively with your heart, and that means more than I can possibly say. And it makes me love you all the more."

His words are beautiful. They speak to my soul, and my soul answers. "Those are the very reasons I love you. You looked past my sightless eyes and really saw me. Until you, no one ever has."

He rests his forehead against mine for a moment in silent contemplation. "Have you ever been kissed, Evangeline?" he whispers, his warm breath fanning my face. "Has a man ever held you this close and tasted your irresistible mouth?"

"No," I softly answer. His words are the most sensual I've ever heard. His fingers continue their exploration of my face and soon his lips follow, kissing a path to mine.

I sigh and my lips part, giving him access that he immediately accepts. The minute his tongue sweeps against mine, the heat of molten lava fills my insides, reaching every part of my body, setting my body on fire. Nothing in life–in this earthly sphere–could have prepared me for the love, the passion, the emotionally-tumultuous ecstasy I am now experiencing at his hands. I cling to him, my hands roaming everywhere, unable to get close enough, every part of me wanting to touch every part of him. I've never felt such longing. I never knew it existed.

"Adagio." In my whispering of his name is an unspoken plea, a need to be closer to him, and it only serves to increase the heat between us. His returning moan and the touch of his hands say what his voice does not.

Breaking the kiss suddenly, he stands and lifts me in his arms and carries me into the house. When the door is closed, I am pressed against the wall and his heated mouth again claims mine. His muscular arms band around my waist, caressing my back. My hands are soon lost in his hair and his kiss sears a burning path to my neck where his mouth makes thorough work of assuring not an inch goes untouched. When my legs can no longer hold me, he locks me securely against him. All coherent thought is gone as he fills my mind, commanding the response of my every sense. I slip a hand under his shirt and the taunt skin on his back is like fire beneath my fingertips. The hunger of his kiss increases, his warm mouth threatening to devour me whole, and I meet that hunger with the voraciousness of my own. Every inch of me burns for him. I have never experienced such burning need. I can't even put it into words. I can't speak, period.

Just when I think I will faint from the heat of his affections and the desire they've lit inside me, his mouth slowly parts from mine. His arms are still around me, his warm breath fanning my face. I can feel his gaze, and I long to know what his face expresses as he looks at me. I *need* to know. My fingers slowly explore his features, his breath hitching once more as they move over his lips. Fingers are quickly replaced by my own lips as I press them to his.

"Will you marry me?" he asks as his mouth lightly moves over mine. "Please say yes." But before I can answer, his kiss deepens, adding new kindling to the already burning fires of my heart.

Pulling back just a little, I say, "Yes." There can be no other answer. After experiencing such beautiful and exquisite passion at his hand, there is no way I can ever be without it again. I can never be away from *him* again.

For a moment we just hold one another, never wanting to let go. Adagio moves back a little, still keeping one arm wrapped around me. "I have something for you." he tells me. Taking my hand, he slips a ring onto my finger. I touch it with my other and gasp.

"But how . . ."

"Come and sit with me, *mi amore*, and I will share the story of this ring and the two amazing women who wore it."

* * *

I have been lying in bed for hours, but I can't seem to fall asleep. My mind is filled with thoughts of Adagio and how quickly he claimed my heart. Over and over the evening we spent together sweeps through my thoughts. Every single moment had been heavenly.

We stayed up until late, wrapped up in one another, sharing kisses and tender caresses, whispering words of love and longing. When we finally said goodnight, it was with painful reluctance, hating to separate even for the short space of time the night takes from us. Everything in me needs to be with him, needs him touching me in some way.

Sighing, I get up and head to the kitchen, deciding a cup of chamomile tea might help. I notice a dim light coming from the living room and I head in that direction.

"Adagio," I whisper.

"I am here, *amore*," he says, taking my hand. "I couldn't sleep," he tells me, guiding me to the couch. He sits down and pulls me onto his lap, linking his arms around me.

"I couldn't sleep either."

"I think we are both suffering from the same love-induced insomnia." By the amused tone of his voice, I can tell he is smiling.

"I think so, too." Resting a hand on his muscular chest, I lay my head against his shoulder, idly running my fingers through his deep waves, taking pleasure in the way his heartbeat speeds up and his lips immediately search for mine. His kiss is pleasurably-slow and gentle. The feel and taste of his mouth is heavenly. My hand roams from his chest to his face and I caress his cheek, smiling against his mouth as his hand becomes buried in my hair.

"Everything about you intoxicates me," he whispers, deepening the kiss. "I don't think I will ever get enough of you." His lips travel to my ear. "Not a minute will go by when I won't need you, when I won't need to touch you, or need you to touch me."

Shivers of pleasure roll through me, producing goosebumps on my arms. His warm hand rubs them away. "I feel the same. I don't think we can get married fast enough."

I feel him smile against my cheek. Grabbing the quilt draped across the arm of the sofa, Adagio moves me from is lap. He puts his feet up and reclines back against one of the throw pillows, drawing me down to lay in front of him, and spreads the quilt over us. Lying in his arms, he pulls me deeper into himself. Linking his fingers through mine, he kisses my ear and whispers, "I love you, baby."

I turn my head, allowing him access to my waiting lips. "I love you, too."

Safe in his embrace, I slowly fall asleep.

Chapter 10

Adagio takes my hand and leads me through the kitchen out to the back yard. "I've made us a picnic."

I smile, squeezing his hand. "Thank you. I've never been on a picnic."

"Somehow I knew you would say that. Woman, you need to get out more." I punch his arm softly and he laughs.

Guiding me to a blanket spread out on the grass, Adagio draws me to the middle and I sit, stretching my legs out in front of me. The afternoon sun is bright and I relish its warmth on my face.

"I have prepared us a fine fare of chicken salad

croissants, homemade sweet potato chips, fresh fruit salad, and lemon crème brulee."

"Mmmm, sounds yummy. My mouth is watering already."

"Mine is as well, only not for food."

"I can help you with that," I say, reaching for him.

We are quickly lying on the blanket wrapped in each other's arms, lunch forgotten for the moment as passion ignites between us. There can't possibly be anyone more gifted with a kiss than Adagio. His lips travel over my brows, my cheeks, my ears, my neck. His mouth is hot against my skin, and when it fully meets mine again, my hand are soon buried in the softness of his wavy hair.

"What do you see when you look at me?" I whisper against his lips.

Drawing back a little, he says, "I see God's perfect gift to me." He touches my face. "I see beautiful caramel skin, lovely brown eyes, and luscious, kissable lips parting in an amazing smile that is just for me. I see the fire in your eyes each time I touch you, and feel your longing each time I kiss you. Everything I see in you, I feel inside my own heart." He rolls me over, holding me against him. "What do you see when you look at me?"

I allow my hands to travel over his handsome features, my fingers lingering against his full lips. "I see love. I see your love for me. I see eyes that I can imagine are looking through me, taking in my every exposed thought, each one of them centered on my love for you. I can picture the desire in your expression when you hold me, touch me, kiss me. And it only serves to feed mine."

I kiss him again and all conversation ceases. We spend most of the day in this spot, talking, laughing and loving. We plan for our marriage and makes decisions about where we will live. There is no question of our living in Italy in his family home and I am excited about the move.

Night falls and loneliness sets in again when I think about saying goodnight him. Then I remind myself that living in his home is better than staying alone at my apartment until we leave in a couple of weeks. I am very grateful to be waking up in the same house. The only thing better than that will be waking up in his arms when we are married. I long for that more than I can say.

We spend the next couple of weeks boxing up my things and putting away what I don't plan to take. We clean out his fridge and mine, grateful that Mother isn't too proud to take the new food we don't want to throw away. She tells me how much she will miss me, and for the first time in my life, I can say the same and mean it.

* * *

On their final evening in the states, Adagio and Evangeline order dinner in and enjoy the coziness of the house. Adagio will indeed miss the place and the memories he and Evangeline have shared there. His grandmother had been right; his life truly started there. He is sure they will come back every now and then, especially since Evangeline's mother will still be here.

Adagio spoons some fried rice onto their plates and adds some shrimp as he talks more about their move.

"Other than my parents, we will be the only ones living in the family villa. After the wedding, they plan to take an extended vacation, visiting the triplets, Marcella, Geneva and Jessica, and their families in Rome, and my sister, Angela, and her family in Greece. So for six months or so, we will have the house completely to ourselves."

Epilogue

Standing on the bedroom balcony of the villa we've rented for our honeymoon, I soak in the warmth of Adagio's arms and ponder the day as we enjoy the night air. Our wedding vows had been spoken on the veranda of the St. John villa and the ceremony was simple but beautiful. Surrounded by Adagio's family, and my mother beside me standing as my maid of honor, we declared our love for each other and became one as we were pronounced husband and wife.

Then, last night we became one flesh as he made love to me, carrying me, in mind and body, to places I never knew existed. The touch of his hands, the passion of his kisses, the heated sensation of his skin against mine . . . there are no words that could do it justice.

"Tell me what you see."

He tightens his embrace, pressing his cheek against mine. "The moon is big and full and lights up the sky. All the stars are out and there are no clouds. The lights of the closer homes filter through the groves, dotting the distance." He quietly contemplates for a moment and I know he is trying to find a way to describe everything since I have no concept of what these things look like. I can see light and dark, and that's it. "Remember what I said I see when I look at you?" he finally asks. "That is the beauty that is before me now, enhanced ten-fold because you are here in my arms. If you were not here with me, it wouldn't be the same." I reach back and caress his cheek as he buries he face in my hair. "My entire being is consumed with you, *mi amore.*"

"And mine with you. Now, what is the surprise you mentioned?"

"Oh, nothing much, just that my grandparents rented this villa years ago, and the room we are staying in was their when they were here."

"Really? Oh, my heck, really?"

"Yes," he answers, laughing at my excitement. "My grandfather wrote about it in my grandmother's journal before she passed away. It is in his as well, but because he knew *Nonna* was leaving hers to me, he added a fully-detailed account."

"Tell me about it," I say, turning to face him.

"Well, they were planning another vacation here at the end of the summer, but there was an accident. I will save that story for my parents to share at another time, but basically the vacation was put off for six months or so because my grandmother was hit by a car and suffered some major injuries. It took a while for her to heal, and even when she did, she had a slight limp for the rest of her life."

"Wow," I whisper, completely awed by this woman. "So they finally made the trip."

"Yes, and while they were here my grandmother shared with my grandfather an experience she had while she was unconscious in the hospital."

"Do you need to grab the journal?"

"No, I remember it word for word."

Dagio, this experience is in my own journal, but

Nonna and I felt that I should include a detailed entry in hers. We know this will mean a great deal to you because you are so much like me–well, like me a few years ago. (Don't laugh.)

We were staying in a villa in Tuscany. Sitting out on the bedroom balcony, your grandmother told me there was something she needed to share with me. She said it was something she has wanted to tell me since the moment she awakened in the hospital, but the time just never felt right.

"What is it?" I asked. She was quiet for a moment, so I silently studied her face.

"I had an amazing experience while I was unconscious. It was brief, but it will stay with me forever. At first I thought maybe it was a dream, but I know without a doubt it was real." She slowly smiled. "I saw your mother, Adagio."

My grip on her hand tightened. "You saw my mother?" My voice was thick with emotion.

"I did. I knew her before she even told me who she was because you look so much like her."

"Tell me, amore. How did she look?"

"She looked beautiful. She was a lovely petite

woman with laughing emerald eyes and a long, dark, thick wavy mane. She was dressed in spotless white and looked like an angel.

"Your description is perfect. I always thought my mother was beautiful. And since you have never seen a picture of her, I have no doubt it was her you saw."

"My time with her was brief, but I remember everything she said to me. I remember the warmth I felt from her. She never touched me, but just being near her was indescribable."

"What did she say?"

"She said she loved me, and you . . . and that our marriage was meant to be. She told me the love we share is the purest kind, and it will never die." She paused and wiped the falling tears from my cheeks. "She said nothing more, but she stayed a little longer until I awakened."

I silently absorbed all she shared with me before reverently telling her, "I am glad you were able to meet my mother and still be here to tell me about it. She is an amazing woman." I pressed a hand to her face. "And so are you." Staring into her eyes, I caressed her cheek and gently took her face between my hands.

"It's frightening, this powerful hold you have on my heart. To love you so much that everything in me aches to be where you are. I have often wondered why sometimes I cannot tell where I end and you begin, how I can feel so connected to you that my every sense is consumed with you. There have been times when my need for you has been so strong, I literally could not think, function, or even breathe unless I had you in my arms."

I traced a caressing finger over her lips. "And when I thought I was going to lose you, I knew I would die. I couldn't have survived. I have asked myself over and over how I can be so integrated with you, how you can be such a part of me that I can't even exist without you." Releasing a shaky breath, I touched my lips to hers, then drew back slightly. "Now I know why. You really are supposed to be mine, amore." I whispered breathlessly against her lips, "Siete stati promessi me. You were promised to me. That is why you are such a part of me. So much so that I can literally feel you moving inside my soul. I know now that my heart has always belonged to you, and it always will. Everything I am is yours, Cisely."

Then there were no more words between us.

I devoured her mouth with a kiss that was demanding, possessive, and infinitely filling at the same time. I was drowning in delirium as her softness and warmth consumed my every sense. I couldn't hold her close enough, couldn't kiss her enough. Each kiss, each moment in her arms, only fueled my burning need for her. I felt like I would die if I waited any longer to make love to her.

I finally drew back and stood, lifting her in my arms. Our gazes were locked as I carried her into the house and our eyes conveyed to each other that no more words were needed.

Dagio, I treasured those days with my sweetheart more than words could ever express.

Warm tears trail down my cheeks, wetting Adagio's bare chest where my face is burrowed. I have never heard anything so stirring. I finally raise my face to his and smile. "I can understand now why you waited so long to marry." I close my eyes as he kisses my brow.

"I just couldn't settle. I needed to feel that way about someone, to have that kind of love." His forehead touches mine. "That is what I have with you."

"And I'm grateful it was me you waited for."

"So am I." He holds me closer and my body molds to his. "I love you, baby," he whispers against my neck, causing my eyes to again slip shut as his loving begins again.

"I love you too," I softly say. He captures my mouth with his, allowing his kisses and caresses to re-stake his claim on my heart, and mine on his. We truly belong to one another, and my home is in his arms. It always has been, and will be forever.

Surely the heavens are smiling upon us.

And I am just as sure Adagio's grandparents are standing in the brightest cheering section.

J. Adams

About the Author

J. (Jewel) Adams stays crazy busy with her family and writing. She has written several books in different genres and is also a motivational speaker to both youth and adult audiences.

In her spare time (when she has any) she likes to curl up with a good book and a healthy stash of orange Tic Tacs. She and her family reside in Utah.

Jewel loves hearing from her fans. You can contact her at jewela40@gmail.com

Visit Jewels Blog at jewelsbestgems.blogspot.com

www.ingramcontent.com/pod-product-compliance
Lightning Source LLC
Chambersburg PA
CBHW070537130626
46555CB00003B/1469